This book
belongs to:

. . . .

Contents

Peppa Goes Camping

Today, Peppa and George are very excited.
They are going on holiday!
Daddy Pig has a surprise.

Honk! Honk!

"It's a camper van," grunts Daddy Pig.

"Wow!" gasp Peppa and George.

"We're going on holiday!" sings Peppa.
"We're going on holiday in our camper van! Snort!"
"Hmmm," says Daddy Pig, looking at the map.

"Daddy Pig!" cries Mummy Pig. "Are we lost?"
"Well, er," begins Daddy Pig. "Yes!"

Grandad Dog and Danny Dog arrive.
"Hello," calls out Peppa. "We're lost!"
"Is your satnav broken?" asks Grandad Dog, confused.

Peppa, George, Mummy and Daddy Pig don't know what a satnav is.

"Satnav is a computer that helps you find your way," explains Grandad Dog.
"Welcome to the car of the future," bleeps the satnav.

"Can you tell us where to go?" asks Peppa.
"Go straight on," replies the satnav.

Daddy Pig thanks Grandad Dog, and the family continue on their way. "We're going on holiday," sings Peppa. "We're going on holiday in our camper van!"

Suddenly the camper van is low on oil.
But Daddy Pig can't find the engine!

Mummy Sheep and Suzy Sheep arrive in their car.
"Hello, Suzy," cries Peppa. "We've lost our engine!"
"Lost your engine?" replies Mummy Sheep.

"I don't know a thing about engines,"
she says. "But I'll have a look."

"I'm probably wrong, but this looks like an engine," says Mummy Sheep, lifting the boot.
"Well spotted, Mummy Sheep," gasps Daddy Pig.

Daddy Pig pours oil into the engine. Glug! Glug! Everyone thanks Mummy Sheep, and the family are off again!

"Are we nearly there yet?" asks Peppa, sighing.
"Just up the next hill," says the satnav.

When they get to the top of a steep hill, the satnav says, "You have reached your destination."
"Hooray!" everyone cheers.

"Time for bed," says Mummy Pig.
Peppa and George put on their pyjamas.
"But where will we sleep?" asks Peppa.

"Mummy Pig and I will sleep on this bed," says Daddy Pig, pressing a button.
Whirrr!

Ta-da! A lovely big bed appears in the room.
"And you two will sleep upstairs, like you always do,"
says Mummy Pig.

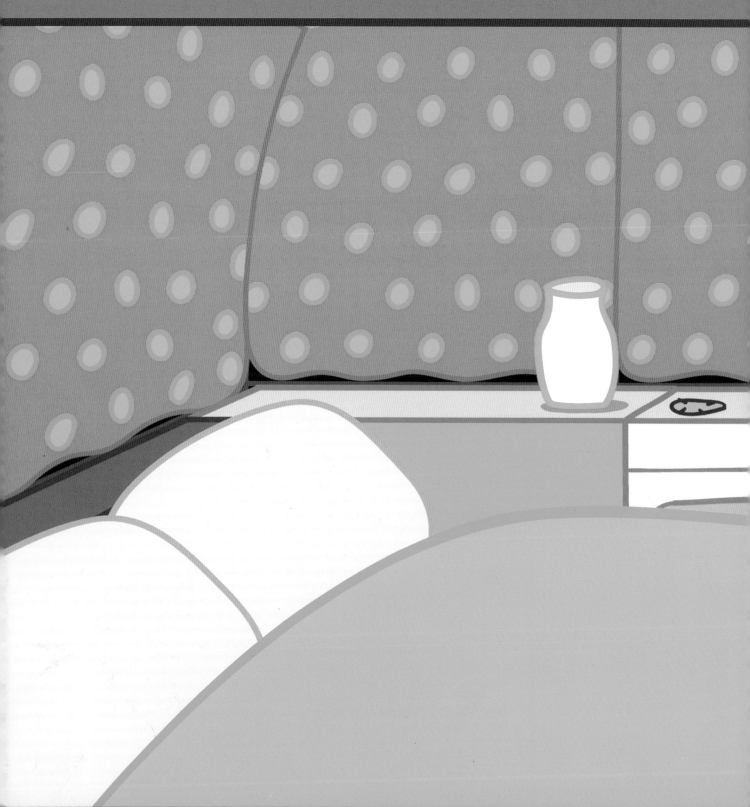

"Watch this," says Daddy Pig, pressing another button.
Whirrr! Click!

Suddenly the roof lifts up and a bunk bed appears.
Daddy Pig tucks Peppa and George into bed.

"The camper van is like our little house!" says Peppa.
"Goodnight, everyone," says the satnav. "Sleep well!"

Peppa Pig's
Family Computer

Mummy Pig is working on the family computer.
She is typing very fast.

Mummy Pig has a lot of important work to do today.

Daddy Pig is in the kitchen making soup for lunch.

"Daddy?" Peppa asks. "Can we go and watch Mummy on the computer, please?"
"Yes, as long as you don't disturb her," Daddy Pig says.

29

"Mummy?" Peppa asks. "Can George and I sit on your lap and watch you work?"

"Yes, as long as you both sit quietly," Mummy Pig agrees.

About a minute later, Peppa asks, "Can we play the Happy Mrs Chicken game on the computer?"

Mummy Pig says, "We can play Happy Mrs Chicken later. But now I have to work."

Another minute later, Peppa asks, "Mummy? Can we help you work?" Peppa taps away at the computer like Mummy Pig.

"No, Peppa!" Mummy says. "You mustn't touch the computer while I'm working."

"Yes, George," Peppa says in a bossy voice.
"You mustn't do this." Peppa taps away again and the computer crashes.

"Peppa! Stop!" Mummy Pig says.
"Sorry, Mummy," Peppa says. "I was just showing George what not to do."

"Daddy Pig!" Mummy calls. "Can you mend the computer while I finish the lunch?"

"Uh . . ." Daddy Pig says. "I'm not very good with these things."

"Hmmm . . ." Daddy Pig pushes a button.
"Mmmm . . ." Daddy Pig pushes another button.

"Maybe if I switch it off and switch it on again . . ."

Daddy Pig has mended the computer!
"Hooray, Daddy!" shouts Peppa.

She and George jump up and down.
"Yes," Daddy Pig smiles. "I am a bit of an expert at these things."

"Daddy," Peppa asks. "Can we play that computer game, Happy Mrs Chicken? Mummy said we could play it later," Peppa says. "And now it's later!"

"Well . . ." Daddy Pig thinks for a moment. "OK then."
Daddy Pig starts the Happy Mrs Chicken game.

"Ho, ho, ho!" Daddy Pig laughs as Peppa and George play Happy Mrs Chicken.

"Snort!" Mummy Pig says as she comes into the room.
"I see the computer is working again!"

Daddy Pig's
Lost Keys

Peppa and her family are on a day trip, visiting the mountains. It's time to go back to the car.

"Thank you for visiting the mountain beauty spot," says Miss Rabbit.

"Key! Key!" snorts George.
"You can't play with the car keys!" laughs Daddy Pig.
"You might lose them."

Daddy Pig can play with the car keys because he's a grown-up.

"Whoops!"
Oh dear. Daddy Pig has dropped the car keys down
a drain.

"Time to go home!" says Mummy Pig.
Daddy Pig goes red. "That might be difficult," he says.

Daddy Pig tries to get the keys out of the drain with
a stick.

"Hmm . . ." he says. "The drain is deeper than
I thought."
The stick is not long enough to reach the keys.

Daddy Pig has a better idea.
"What we need is a fishing rod!"
So he buys one from Miss Rabbit.

Daddy Pig's idea doesn't work. The fishing line is not long enough to reach the keys.

Mr Bull and his friends arrive.
They've come to enjoy the quiet beauty spot.
"It's our day off!" shouts Mr Bull.

Mr Bull talks very loudly.
"Er, Mr Bull?" asks Daddy Pig. "Could we borrow your crane for a minute to rescue my keys?"

"Say no more," cries Mr Bull. "We'll have your keys out in no time!"

64

Mr Rhino gets to work, but it's no good. Even the crane can't reach the keys!

"Now what shall we do?" wonders Daddy Pig.

Chug! Chug! Chug!

"Easy!" shouts Mr Bull. "We'll dig up the road!"

The crew dig up the beauty spot.
Mr Bull is lowered all the way down to the bottom of the hole.

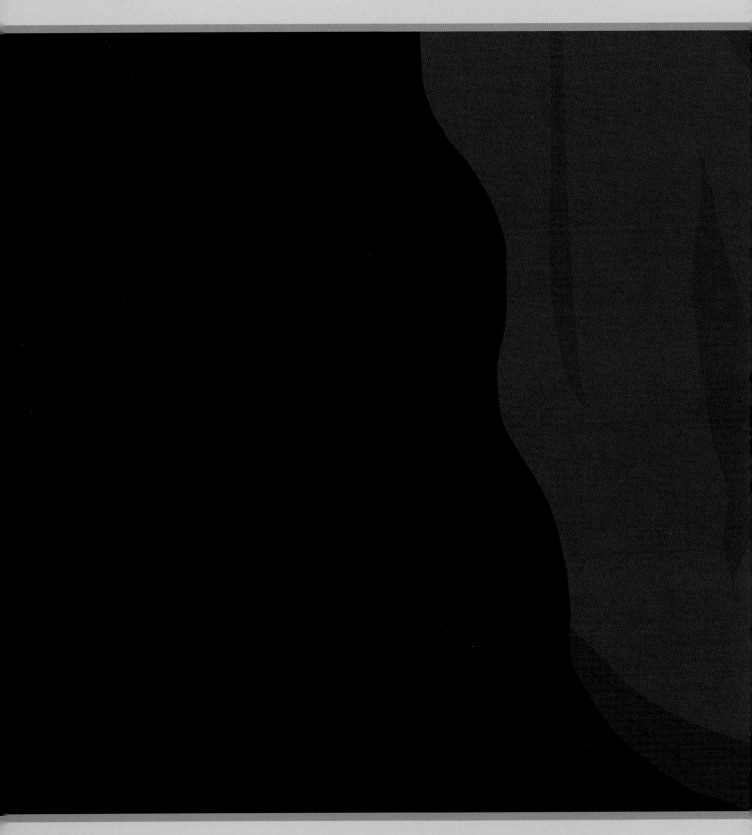

"Here are the keys!" he bellows.
"We've got them!"

Now there is a big hole in the mountain beauty spot. It is a cave beauty spot instead.

"And it's all thanks to my daddy!" giggles Peppa.

Miss Rabbit's
Day Off

Peppa, George and Suzy Sheep have had a sleepover at Rebecca Rabbit's house.

"It's fun having carrots for breakfast!" laughs Peppa.
"I could eat carrots all day!" agrees Daddy Rabbit.

Mummy Rabbit's sister, Miss Rabbit, pops in to say hello.

"I can't stop long," she says. "I've got lots of work to do. I'm working at the supermarket, selling ice creams and driving the bus!"

Miss Rabbit trips over one of Richard's toys.
Her ankle is hurt.

"You must stay here and get better," decides Mummy Rabbit. "I'll do your work for you."

Oww!

Mummy Rabbit puts Rebecca and her friends in charge of looking after Miss Rabbit.

Luckily, Suzy Sheep has her nurse's outfit with her.
"Don't worry," she says. "I am only a pretend nurse!"

Mummy Rabbit goes straight to the supermarket. "Miss Rabbit is ill," she tells everyone. "I'll be doing her job today."

"Have you ever worked a checkout before?" asks
Mrs Dog.
Mummy Rabbit has not.

Running a supermarket checkout is quite hard.
Mrs Rabbit calls home.

"We need more help!" she cries. "This job is going to take me all day!"

Peppa phones Miss Rabbit's ice cream stall.
Daddy Pig answers.
"Miss Rabbit is ill. You've got to sell the ice cream today!"

"Ho, ho!" snorts Daddy Pig. "I'm an expert at ice cream!" He gets to work.

Selling ice cream is quite hard.
Soon the ice cream begins to melt.

The ice cream is all runny.
"Ice cream soup, anyone?" asks Daddy Pig.

Peppa phones Grandad Dog.
"Miss Rabbit is very ill. Can you drive her bus today please?"

Grandad Dog gets to work, but driving a bus is quite hard. It is even harder when you have cars to fix, too.

Back at Rebecca Rabbit's house, Miss Rabbit is feeling better.

"Can I get up now?" she asks.
Suzy Sheep shakes her head. "No! You must lie very
still . . . but please keep breathing."

"It's not easy doing all your jobs," says Mummy Rabbit at the end of the day.

"It's not easy sitting down all day!" says Miss Rabbit.
She will definitely be back at work tomorrow!

George's First Day
at Playgroup

Today is George's first day at playgroup.
"Isn't George too small for playgroup?" asks Peppa.
"You can look after him," says Daddy Pig.

Peppa isn't sure she wants George at **her** playgroup, but she likes the idea of looking after him.

"Are you sure George is big enough?" Peppa asks when they arrive.
"Yes, he'll be fine," replies Daddy Pig.

"OK. He can come," says Peppa.
She holds on to George's hand.
"Grunt! Grunt!" snorts George, jumping up and down.

Here is Madame Gazelle, Peppa's playgroup teacher. She looks after Peppa and her friends. Madame Gazelle tells the children that George is coming to play.

The children are all very excited about meeting Peppa's little brother.

"This is my little brother, George," cries Peppa.
"Grrr! Dine-saw!" growls George.
"Hee! Hee! Hee!" everyone laughs.

"I wish I had a little brother like George,"
baas Suzy Sheep.

George shakes his toy, Mr Dinosaur, at Madame
Gazelle. "Grrr! Dine-saw!"
"Aah! Really scary!" Madame Gazelle laughs.

Peppa is proud of George making everyone laugh. "George is my little brother. He's brilliant," she says.

"Shall we show George how we paint pictures?"
Madame Gazelle asks the children.

"George is not very good at painting," says Peppa.
"But I can show him how to paint a flower."

"Watch me, George," snorts Peppa. "First, you paint a big circle."

Peppa carefully dips her brush into a pot of pink paint and draws a big pink circle right in the middle of her paper.

George draws a big green circle.
"No, George. That's the wrong colour,"
snorts Peppa. "Watch me."

Peppa makes yellow petal shapes.
George paints a green zigzag.
"George! That's the wrong shape," says Peppa.

Peppa admires her flower painting.
"Perfect," she says happily.
George is still painting.

Instead of a stalk and leaves, he has painted another
circle with five lines sticking out from it.
"You are doing it all wrong!" says Peppa.

"I've painted a flower," says Peppa.
"Very good, Peppa," says Madame Gazelle. "And look,
George has painted a dinosaur."

Madame Gazelle sticks Peppa and George's pictures on the wall.

Now it is time to go home.
"What will you paint next time, George?" asks
Madame Gazelle.

"Dine-saw! Grrr!" George giggles.
"Hee! Hee! Hee!" everyone laughs.

Peppa's First
Sleepover

Peppa is going to her very first sleepover at Zoe Zebra's house. "Welcome to my sleepover!" Zoe says.

"I'll pick you up in the morning," Mummy Pig says to Peppa with a kiss.

Rebecca Rabbit, Suzy Sheep and Emily Elephant are already here.
"I've got my teddy," Peppa says.

Zoe has her monkey. Rebecca has her carrot.
Suzy has her owl. And Emily has her frog.

"Don't stay up too late, girls! And don't be too loud. Daddy Zebra has to get up early to deliver the post," Mummy Zebra says as she turns out the lights.

Zoe's baby twin sisters, Zuzu and Zaza, want to join the sleepover too.
"Sleepovers are only for big girls!" Zoe says.

The twins begin to cry.
"They're so sweet and little," Peppa says.

"Can they stay?" Rebecca asks.
"OK," Zoe says to the twins. "But you must NOT fall asleep."

"What should we do first?" Suzy asks.
"I'm having piano lessons!" says Zoe. "Listen . . ."

Zoe starts to pound on the keys.
"Twinkle, twinkle, little star . . ."

Mummy Zebra has woken up.
"Shush! You must be quiet so Daddy Zebra can sleep!
Now, into your sleeping bags, please."

"Snort! What do we do now?" Peppa asks.
"At sleepovers, there's always a midnight
feast!" Zoe says.

"It's when we eat things," Suzy says
in a hushed voice, "in secret."

"Shhh!" Zoe says as she leads the girls to the kitchen. They each grab some delicious fruit, perfect for a midnight feast.

The floorboard creaks.

Oh no! Mummy Zebra has woken up. "You'll wake Daddy Zebra! Now, who knows a bedtime story?"
"Once upon a time, there was a fairy . . ." Suzy begins.

"And she lived in the forest . . ." Peppa continues.
"And the fairy met a big monster, who went . . . RAARRR!"
Emily says with a big elephant trumpet noise!

Oh dear. The noise has woken Daddy Zebra!
"Sorry, Daddy," Zoe says. "There was a story about a fairy and a scary monster."

"And we want to know what happens next!" Peppa says.
"Very well," Daddy Zebra sighs. "The monster lifted up
his great, big hairy paws . . ."

"And walked along on his great, big hairy feet . . . And sang . . . 'Twinkle, twinkle, little star, how I wonder what you are . . .'"

Daddy Zebra sings gently as he plays the piano.
Daddy Zebra's song has sent everyone to sleep.